GET SET
TO WRECK!

Written and illustrated by
Robin Rector Krupp

Four Winds Press
New York

For Meredith Charpentier
a multistoried book builder

Four Winds Press, Macmillan Publishing Company
866 Third Avenue, New York, NY 10022
Collier Macmillan Canada, Inc.
Printed and bound by South China Printing Company,
Hong Kong. First American Edition

10 9 8 7 6 5 4 3 2 1

The text of this book is set in 14 pt. Century Schoolbook.
The illustrations are rendered in pencil, gouache, pastel,
and colored pencil on white and colored paper.

Library of Congress Cataloging-in-Publication Data
Krupp, Robin Rector.   Get set to wreck!
Summary: While struggling to learn his vowels, a young boy
imagines that they come to life to help him understand
them better.
[1. English language–Vowels–Fiction] I. Title.
PZ7.K94625Ge 1988 [E] 86-19956
ISBN 0-02-751140-5

"Oh, no!" said Curtis. "Not now! I'm almost ready to knock this down. And that's the best part! Anyway, that homework's too hard.

"It's on vowels!" he howled. "And I don't know them all yet. Just look at these instructions."

Name:

Homework

The vowels are **A, E, I, O, U,** and sometimes **Y**. List at least three words for each of the five long and short vowels. Use your imagination!

Long Vowels

Short Vowels

Ă

Ē

Ĕ

Ī

Ĭ

Ō

Ŏ

Ū

Ŭ

Ā

"Use my imagination? That works for vowels? Well, I don't think so," he said, "but I'll try it. Short **A**, short **A**, what does it sound like? I need three words for short **A**." Curtis closed his eyes.

Nothing happened.

Still nothing happened.

Then he thought he saw something fuzzy.

Short **A** was standing among the tall letters. Short **A** whispered, "Action, hammer, and hat. I'm in all those words. Go on, imagine us. Give us a chance."

Curtis forgot about being angry.

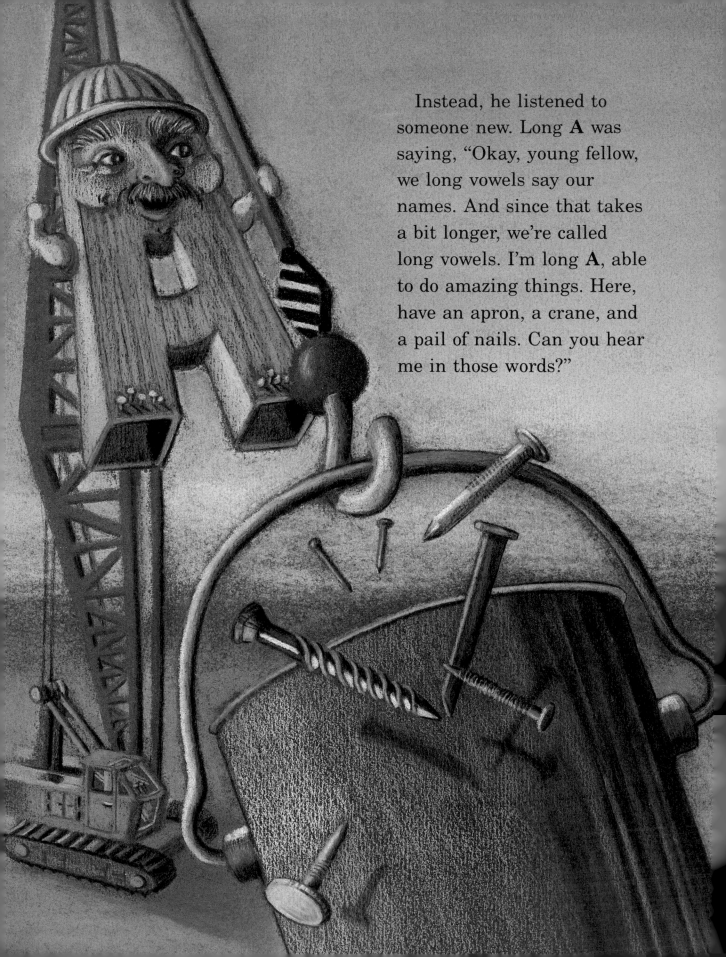

Instead, he listened to someone new. Long **A** was saying, "Okay, young fellow, we long vowels say our names. And since that takes a bit longer, we're called long vowels. I'm long **A**, able to do amazing things. Here, have an apron, a crane, and a pail of nails. Can you hear me in those words?"

Curtis said, "But this is all so crazy."

Long **A** laughed. "Say, there's a long **A** in the word crazy, too. I think you're getting the right idea."

But Curtis was getting another idea. "I might be able to work with these guys. I wonder who's next?"

Hundreds of short **E**s sped in.

"Want to help me build something?" Curtis asked.

"Help? You bet!" they said.

Now Curtis was getting excited. Anything was possible.

Short **E** said, "Put it up and we'll take it down. With short **E** you get energy, explosions, and demolition."

Curtis yelled …

Screech! Long **E** was even more eager. "How about me? Can you hear me in equal, wheels, and feet? Anyway, you need me to read."

Curtis said, "Aw, what do I need to read?"

"This," said short I.
"Instructions and building
permits."

"That's it!" said Curtis,
getting inspired. "What will
we build?"

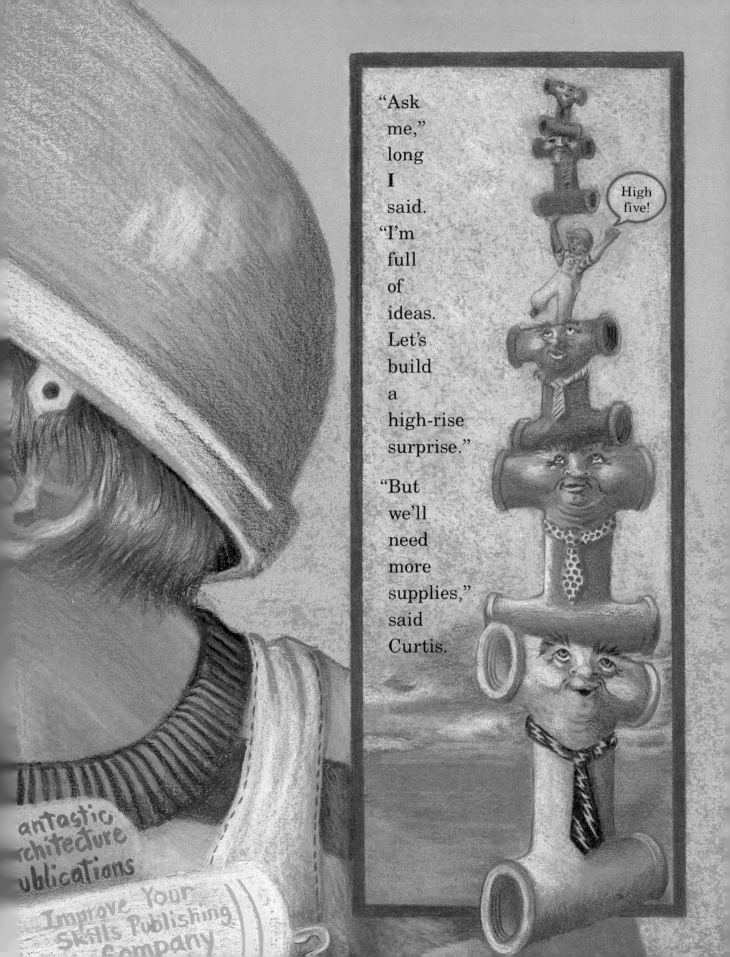

"I'll keep you occupied," short **O** said. "I've got boxes of blocks. Did you hear me in those words?"

"Gosh, I did," said Curtis, "and here are a few more. Let's not stop until we reach the top!"

Finally, Curtis came to long **O**. "Oh, no! We're nowhere near the top. This is going so slow. I want to get to the best part.

"Hey, long **O**, those bulldozers, backhoes, and loaders were late! How will we ever finish?"

Short **U** had the answer.
"With a little luck, lumber,
and trucks. That's what we
need to finish this up."

Long **U** arrived in uniform. Curtis peered
over the ledge. He was ready with some
long **U** words of his own. "I'm so glad to see
you. Can you give the final inspection? We
used all your rules and regulations."

The inspection was passed. The work was done. "Great job, vowels!" said Curtis. "What a good team we make. We'll go on to bigger and better things. But first, get ready for my favorite part!"

"Now you're the **A, E, I, O,** U Demolition Crew.

Curtis! Did you do your homework?

Name: Curtis

Homework

The vowels are **A, E, I, O, U,** and sometimes **Y**. List at least three words for each of the five long and short vowels. Use your imagination!

Short Vowels

Ă
standing, action, hammer, hat, imagine, chance, angry

Ĕ
rescue, mess best yes silent
hundreds, sped, help, bet, getting, excited, get, energy, explosions, demolition, yelled, heck, wreck, set,

Ĭ
this, instructions, building, permits, it, Curtis, getting inspired will, build, operating, forklift, whiz, amazing, weird, things, is, limit, becoming, architect, simple, fantastic, architecture, improve, skills, buildings, publishing

Ŏ
occupied, got, boxes, of, blocks, gosh, not, stop, top

Ŭ
luck, lumber, trucks, up lucky

Long Vowels

Ā
saying, okay, say, names, takes, a, able, amazing, apron, crane, pail, nails, crazy

Ē
screech, even, eager, me, equal, wheels, feet, need, read

Ī
I'm, ideas, high-rise, surprise, supplies, high, five

Ō
Oh, no, nowhere, going, so, slow, won't, go, those, bulldozers, backhoes, loaders, tow, know

Ū
uniform, you, used, rules, regulations, rule

"Oh, yeah! It was fun! Look at all I've done … **A, E, I, O, U** …

... and sometimes **Y** as in good-bye!"